Strawberry Shortcake
and the
Friendship Party

Grosset & Dunlap

ISBN 0-448-43222-6   A B C D E F G H I J

Strawberry Shortcake
and the
Friendship Party

By Monique Z. Stephens
Illustrated by Carolyn Bracken

Grosset & Dunlap • New York

One day, Strawberry Shortcake and her little sister, Apple Dumplin', were looking through a photo album. It was full of pictures of their best friends.

"I always have such *berry* fun times with my friends," Strawberry said. "I wish I could show them how much they mean to me.

"I know!" Strawberry exclaimed. "I'll have a party for all of my friends!"

Strawberry Shortcake quickly got out her art supplies and made some invitations.

You're invited!
Please come to my first-ever
Friendship Party,
this Saturday at two o'clock.
Check below to let me know
if you can come.

☐ Yes, I'm coming! ☺
☐ Sorry, I can't make it. ☹

"There!" Strawberry said happily when she had finished the
cards. "I have invitations for each of my friends—Orange Blossom,
Huckleberry Pie, Ginger Snap, Honey Pie Pony, and Angel Cake!
Now all I have to do is deliver them."

Strawberry Shortcake carefully tucked the invitations in her pocket. But as soon as Strawberry and Apple walked outside, a strong gust of wind came and almost knocked them down!

"I can't take Apple Dumplin' out in this weather!" Strawberry said with a frown.

Just then, Honey Pie Pony came trotting down the Berry Trail.

"Hi, Strawberry!" said Honey. "Where are you going?"

"Well, I was going to deliver invitations to my friendship party," Strawberry Shortcake said. "But it's so windy out, I think I'll have to wait until tomorrow."

"Invitations? Party?" Honey said. "I love a good party! If it were me, I wouldn't let a little wind get in the way of my party. Why, when I delivered mail for the Queen, I traveled through rain, sleet, and snow to get the job done! Here, give me the invitations. I'll deliver them for you."

"Oh, Honey, you're the best!" said Strawberry Shortcake. "Thank you *berry* much!" She put four of the invitations inside Honey's saddlebag, and then handed the last one to Honey.

"An invitation for me?" Honey asked. "Thanks, Strawberry! I've never been to a friendship party before!"

As Honey trotted down the Berry Trail, a strong gust of wind lifted the flap of her saddlebag. Strawberry's party invitations went flying everywhere!

"Oh, no!" cried Honey. She galloped back and forth, trying to catch the invitations as they swirled in the wind. She found

one in the low branches of a tree, plucked another from a bird's nest, and chased a third down the road.

"Phew! I think I've finally got them all!" Honey said. She tucked the invitations safely in her bag and then set off again to deliver them.

The next day, Orange Blossom, Huckleberry Pie, and Ginger Snap all stopped by Strawberry's house to tell her they could come to the party.

"Thanks for responding so quickly, everybody," Strawberry said. "I can't wait for the party! See you on Saturday!"

"Honey, Orange Blossom, Ginger Snap, and Huckleberry Pie are all coming to my party!" Strawberry said happily. Then she frowned. "But I haven't heard from Angel Cake yet. Oh, well—I bet she's on her way over right now to tell me she can come."

Strawberry waited for Angel Cake, but she never came over.

Later that afternoon, Orange Blossom stopped by Angel's cake shop.

"Hi, Orange Blossom!" said Angel Cake. "Did you come over to play?"

Orange Blossom shook her head. "I can't today—I have to pick some oranges from my orchard," she said. "I want to order cupcakes for Strawberry's friendship party. Bring them over on Saturday and we can go to the party together, okay? See you then!"

Orange Blossom gave Angel a friendly wave and left.

"Strawberry's having a *friendship* party?" Angel said sadly.
"Why didn't she invite me?"

For two whole days, Angel tried to figure out why she hadn't been invited to Strawberry Shortcake's party. *Is Strawberry mad at me?* Angel wondered. *Did I do something wrong?*

On Saturday, Angel slowly walked over to Orange Blossom's tree house to deliver the cupcakes.

"Thanks, Angel!" Orange Blossom said with a big smile. "Your strawberry cupcakes are Strawberry's favorite kind. Ready to go to the party?"

"No, I'm not going," Angel Cake said sadly.

"Why not?" Orange Blossom asked, surprised.

"Because Strawberry didn't invite me!" replied Angel Cake with tears in her eyes.

"But there must be some mistake!" Orange Blossom said. "It's a *friendship* party, and you're one of Strawberry's berry *best* friends. Come to the party with me so we can ask her what happened."

Angel shook her head. "No way! I can't go to the party if I wasn't invited!" she said in a firm voice.

"I guess we're not such good friends after all," Angel said sadly.

Orange Blossom walked over to Strawberry's house.

"Oh, good, Orange Blossom's here!" Huckleberry Pie said. "Now we're just waiting for Angel Cake. Then the party can start!"

Strawberry shook her head sadly. "I don't think Angel is coming. I haven't seen her in days. And she didn't let me know she couldn't come to my party."

"But Angel Cake thinks she wasn't invited!" exclaimed
Orange Blossom.

"What?" Strawberry asked, looking confused. "Why
would she think that? I sent her an invitation! Honey
delivered it for me."

"Oh, no!" Honey cried suddenly.

"What's wrong, Honey?" asked Strawberry Shortcake.

"I just realized that I *didn't* deliver an invitation to Angel Cake!" Honey said quickly. "There was this big gust of wind and the invitations went flying *everywhere*. I thought I got them all, but I must have missed Angel Cake's invitation. I'm sorry, Strawberry."

"That's okay, Honey," Strawberry Shortcake replied. "It was just a mistake. But poor Angel Cake! She must feel so upset about being left out. I have to go to her house right now to explain what happened!"

"And I'm coming with you!" said Honey.

The two friends set off for Angel Cake's house. On the way, Strawberry Shortcake spotted a tattered piece of paper caught in a bush.

"Look—it's Angel's invitation!" exclaimed Strawberry. Honey quickly picked it up. "This time, I'll make sure Angel gets her invitation!" she said.

Soon Strawberry Shortcake and Honey
arrived at Angel Cake's house.
"What are you doing here?" Angel Cake
asked when she opened the door.

"Oh, Angel Cake, how could you ever think I would have a party and not invite you?" said Strawberry, giving Angel Cake a big hug.

Honey explained what had happened. "I'm really sorry you felt left out, Angel. It was a big mistake!"

Angel smiled at her friends. "And *I'm* sorry I didn't listen to Orange Blossom and just ask you about the party. I should have known that you would never hurt my feelings on purpose."

"Of course I wouldn't!" said Strawberry Shortcake. "Now let's hurry over to my house—we don't want to miss the friendship party!"

When Strawberry Shortcake, Angel Cake, and Honey arrived at the party, everyone clapped and cheered.

"So, are you friends again?" Orange Blossom asked with a smile.

Angel Cake laughed. "We were *always* friends," she said happily.

Strawberry put her arm around Angel's shoulder. "And we always will be!"